CW00418243

The Machine

A short story

Geoff A. Wilson

kindle direct publishing

kindle direct publishing

First published 2021
Kindle Direct Publishing (UK Office)
44 Ashbourne Drive
Coxhoe
DH6 4SW

Edited by Olivia J. Wilson
Cover design software by Canva

About the author

Born in London to a British father and a French mother, **Geoff A. Wilson** grew up in southern Germany where he went to primary and secondary school. He is trilingual in German, French and English. He studied for his MA in Geography, Cultural Anthropology and Archaeology at the University of Freiburg (southern Germany), before completing his PhD in Geography at the University of Otago in Dunedin, New Zealand. From 1992-2003 he worked as a Geography Lecturer/Senior lecturer at King's College London, and from 2004-2019 as Professor of Geography (Emeritus Professor since 2019) at the University of Plymouth (south-west UK). Geoff became a world-renowned academic expert on questions about the resilience of human communities, more specifically about how rural communities cope with, and adapt to, change, disturbances and disasters. He has published over 100 academic articles on the subject and has written several books including *Environmental management: new directions for the 21st century* (with Raymond L. Bryant; UCL Press, 1997), *Multifunctional agriculture: a transition theory perspective* (CABI International, 2007) and *Community resilience and environmental transitions* (Routledge, 2012). Married and with one son, he lives in a small village on the south coast of Devon, UK. Geoff retired in 2019 to become a full-time writer (six novels so far). He specialises in psychological thrillers, young adult fantasy books and dystopian novels. *The machine* is his first short story.

Books by Geoff A. Wilson:

The 'Lllobillo Children's fantasy series':

Lllobillo: The Secret Portal (Austin Macauley, 2017)

The Viking Curse (KDP Publishing, 2020)

Psychological thrillers/Psychological fantasy:

Depravity: A Story About the Darkness of the Human Soul (KDP Publishing, 2020)

Meltdown: The Story of a Tragic Psychological Collapse (KDP Publishing, 2021)

The Dream (KDP Publishing, 2021)

Dystopian fiction:

Pandemic (KDP Publishing, 2020)

Short stories:

The Machine (KDP Publishing, 2021)

Check out Geoff's YouTube channel (you can find it under 'Geoff A. Wilson') where he talks in short videos about his book writing strategy and each of his books

To Franz Kafka

1

Joe Smith woke up with a start. He opened his eyes, but it was pitch black around him. What a terrible nightmare he'd just had! He had never been so scared in his life. He was bathed in sweat and lay askance on his crumpled bedsheet. But although he had only just woken up, he could no longer remember what he had dreamt about, only that it had been the worst nightmare he'd ever had. The memory had vanished in a haze although it had so spooked him.

With echoes of the nightmare raging in his head, he was so afraid that he lay awake for a long time, unable to move, clutching his sweat-soaked bedsheet to his chest as if to protect himself from something lurking in the dark. For a long time he shook with fear. Images flashed through his mind, reminding him of the time when, as a child, he'd had a bad spell of nightmares that prevented him from sleeping properly for years, and how his overworked parents had ignored him when he woke up crying, lying in a puddle of piss from his fear-induced bed-wetting. His awful hare lip was the main reason for his nightmares at the time, his dreams showing him demonic misshapen beings staring at him angrily.

But this last nightmare had not been about his hare lip. It had been about something much deeper, nastier, more terrifying. Maybe the nightmare had been so awful that he did not want to remember it, maybe his brain had automatically switched itself off to protect him? If only he had somebody he could cling to, just anybody to ward off the fear, but he was all alone, and had been for years.

After several minutes of sitting upright in his bed in the dark, dead stiff and not daring to move, soaked in cold sweat and desperately clutching his bedsheet, Joe finally mustered the courage to switch on his bedside lamp, although it took him a while to find the switch in the pitch black with his trembling fingers. Like a stunned animal caught in a car's full-beam headlights, he looked around his small bedsit flat. He was still spooked by the receding tendrils of this awful nightmare. In the dim light it did not take him long to make out the contours of his flat, which comprised only one shabby and dingy room which served him as a bedroom, lounge, and dining room, with his bed tucked into one corner of the room. The dim light cast gloomy shadows over the small kitchenette in the far corner opposite his bed, with a second-hand grimy sink, an old-fashioned electric element which he mainly used to heat up boring and bland tinned food, and an ancient small fridge that made regular croaking and grinding noises when the poorly adjusted thermostat switched on to refrigeration mode.

In the dim light he could just make out the shape of the half-open bathroom door in the corner of the room to his far right. The darkness of the bathroom space behind the door was gawping at him threateningly, reminding him of childhood memories of evil creatures lurking behind an impenetrable blackness. Although he was still stiff with fear from the receding nightmare, he could smell the damp rot and mould wafting towards him from the bathroom.

He looked around the room while the last remnants of his awful nightmare finally dissipated into a haze of ignorance. What had he dreamt that had so frightened and upset him? While clutching the sheet tighter to his chest he racked his brain again, but could not remember anything about the dream. Only that it had been truly awful and that it had scared him to death. He looked around the room in the faint yellowish light of his bedside lamp, but could not see anything unusual that may might have triggered the nightmare. The sickening but familiar humming of the fridge could be heard, and somewhere above him one of his neighbours was flushing a toilet, the noise of which reverberated through the old pipes like the final hiss of a mortally ill tuberculosis patient. But these were all familiar noises he was used to in this awful, decrepit and falling-apart council housing estate, located in a run-down part of Brixton just south of the Thames not far from central London.

2

After what felt like an eternity, Joe finally untangled himself from the crumpled and damp bedsheet, got up and shuffled towards the bathroom. He could not locate his old and worn slippers (they were probably hiding again somewhere under his bed), and, as a result, he keenly felt the coldness of the floor and the unevenness of the old floorboards through the soles of his thin, blue-veined bare feet that had not seen the sun for years. His feet felt even colder on the cracked tiles of the tiny bathroom.

While he took off his sweat-soaked pyjamas, he avoided, as usual, looking at his face in the bathroom mirror. He did not want to be reminded of the result of a botched operation on his hare lip, an operation his parents had forced on him when he was 16. He knew that the large, red, swollen and lumpy scar on his upper lip looked awful, and that the scar tissue had amplified an already existing speech impediment caused by his cleft upper palate. As a result of both his hare lip and the botched operation, instead of speaking properly Joe always mumbled. When he was with people he had also developed the unfortunate habit of placing a hand in front of his mouth, so that people would not see the dreadful scar. This exacerbated his mumbling as people could not see his lips move.

The outcome had been, that, since childhood, Joe had avoided people and had chosen the life of a loner. After he had left home, his family had also shunned him, further worsening his sense of isolation. Inadvertently, he had chosen a life where he had desperately avoided speaking to and socialising with others, because he felt that all people did was stare endlessly at the awful scar on his upper lip and laugh at his inaudible mumbling. As a result, he never had made friends and, at age 38, had never kissed or been with a girl. He was keenly aware that this was one of the key reasons why he so often felt miserable, lonely and depressed.

Supressing tears at the thought of his miserable life, Joe stepped into the shower. The pipes groaned like a deadly wounded animal as he turned on the hot water tap. As usual, it took nearly a minute until the ice-cold water turned to a tepid drizzle, barely wetting his body. He hated this shower, he hated this decrepit flat, but this time he did not care. He just wanted to wash off the cold sweat that was still clinging to his body like elemental slime, wash off the remnants of this awful nightmare that had scared him to death. He knew that he should not take a shower in the middle of the night, as the singing and whizzing of the old pipes would wake up his neighbours and lead to more complaints about his 'unneighbourly' behaviour, but at this point in time he could not care less. In the wake of this awful nightmare, he had other things to worry about.

Joe felt better after his shower and after putting on a fresh t-shirt (he only owned one pyjama, which now lay, sweat-soaked, in the dirty-clothes basket), but he still had a strange feeling that something was not quite right. Without a further glance at the dimly lit room, he went back to bed and switched off the bedside light. But he kept tossing and turning, and found it hard to get back to sleep. He was worried that the nightmare would resume and haunt him for the rest of the night. Dozing, he kept listening out for strange noises. Every little rustle, whizz or buzz in the old pipes and the fridge jolted him awake repeatedly and he would sit bolt upright in his bed. The rest of the night was a tussle between fitful bursts of restless sleep, noises waking him up, sitting up in bed, staring into the dark for what seemed like hours, and finally slumping back down to sleep, his body utterly tired and exhausted.

3

When his old alarm clock woke him up as usual at 6 am Joe was exhausted. But seeing the hazy daylight seep through the dirty window, the nightmare now seemed like a distant memory. He wondered what the fuss had all been about last night and, indeed, why he had been so scared. He even managed a wry smile when thinking about his strange and scared behaviour, especially about taking a shower in the middle of the night. *What was that all about?*, he thought while shaking his head, berating himself for his odd behaviour.

With limbs aching he crawled out of bed, and suddenly he saw *it*. A machine stood in the middle of his room, the sparse rays of light glancing off its sleek and shiny grey metallic surface. It was about one metre high, perfectly square, and stood on a small quadratic stand. Sitting on the edge of his bed, Joe did not dare to move. How had this thing got into his bedsit? He was sure that when he got up in the middle of the night to take a shower, the machine had not been there. Or had he simply not seen it then in the dim light cast by his bedside light? But the machine stood in the middle of the room, so, surely, he would have seen, or stumbled into it, it if it had been there in the night? Was this thing possibly linked to the terrible nightmare he'd had? Joe rubbed his tired eyes and tried again desperately to remember what he had dreamt, but to no avail.

Suddenly it dawned on Joe that whoever had put the machine there – and they must be at least two people as the machine looked heavy – might still be in his flat. He quickly made his way to the bathroom, the only space in his bedsit that was hidden from view, but the bathroom was empty. Joe also checked the front door, but the top and bottom bolt locks were still firmly in place as he had left them when he had locked the door last evening, and the main lock was also still firmly locked. How had those who had placed the machine in his room got in?

He opened the front door and, conscious that he was only wearing a t-shirt and nothing else, he peered out of the door at the outside landing that linked the various flats on his floor to the staircase. But there was nobody there. It was still early and most of his neighbours were in their beds at this time, as they were either unemployed with no motivation to get up, or too drunk or full of drugs to get out of bed this early in the morning. He scanned the far end of the landing that led to the dimly lit staircase, but other than the ubiquitous graffiti, discarded bits of rubbish, and puddles of piss, there was nothing to be seen. Whoever had placed the machine in his room was gone.

Joe closed the front door and turned his attention to the machine. His room was poorly lit, as the sole grimy window overlooked a desolate, dark and dank backyard surrounded by other decrepit blocks of flats that blocked off the sun for most of the day. He turned on the naked lightbulb, which hung from a precariously frayed wire from the middle of the ceiling, to cast more light on the machine. Only now did Joe become aware of the unusual metallic surface of the machine. In the dim light, the machine seemed to glow faintly from within.

4

Joe rubbed his eyes again, just to make sure that this was not an illusion. He re-opened his eyes. No, the machine was still there in the middle of the room, glaring at him with its dull, matt and sinister sheen. He was not imagining things! He walked towards the machine, but hesitated in respectful distance. Slowly and warily, he moved closer to touching distance and looked down at the top of the machine, which was at the level of his belly button. The machine was open at the top, with a gaping hole about 70 cm wide, occupying most of the top with a relatively sharp rim all around the hole. Joe carefully bent forward and stared into the opening, but all he could see was pitch black nothingness. Suddenly, he felt very cold just standing there in his t-shirt. He hugged himself to ward off the dank chill that crept up his body, but this did not stop the feeling of intense malaise. Staring into the hole, he felt as if he was looking at eternity, as he could see absolutely nothing, not even the sides of the hole, let alone the bottom. The blackness gaping at him looked almost unreal, with no edges and no end. What was this? How was this possible? He had never seen anything like it, and why had this machine appeared suddenly in his room? What did it all mean?

With one hand, Joe tentatively touched the metallic side of the machine. It felt cold and slightly rough. With a shudder Joe imagined shark skin feeling like this, although he had never actually felt the skin of a shark in real life. The surface looked metallic, but he was not sure whether the cold, strange material was metal or something entirely different. Maybe it was one of these new-fangled materials scientists seemed to develop all the time in secretive labs hidden deep underground? Was he part of some kind of government experiment, he wondered, looking again around him, scared and expecting hazmat-suited scientists to suddenly jump out from dark corners of his room. But he knew that was nonsense. As he had ascertained just moments earlier, his flat had been locked all night. It would have been impossible for anyone to come in and dump this machine here without him noticing.

Joe looked at his watch and realised that it was getting late. He had to get ready for work. He tried to prise himself from the machine, but somehow he found it hard to walk away from it. The machine seemed to keep him rooted to the spot like a magnet. He finally tore himself away, put on his clothes and quickly swallowed down a meagre breakfast. But not once did he take his eyes off the machine. There was something about it, a strange metallic allure, an unfathomable attraction, that drew him to it. But he could not be late. Never in his job had he been late for work or missed a day of work because of illness.

5

At work, time seemed to crawl. Joe could not stop thinking about the machine sitting in his room, alluring, beckoning him. Who had put it there? Should he tell his landlord? But the landlord would not care at all, he was a disgusting man who despised Joe. But knowing that, at day's end, he would get back to the mysterious machine, made the whole day feel different. Indeed, Joe's menial and degrading work as a toilet attendant (or 'sanitation worker' in today's idiotically sanitised and politically correct world) in the centre of Brixton, where he was in sole charge of 14 public toilets containing 56 toilet cubicles and 42 urinals, seemed less vile and depressing.

Although Joe had never been very bright, his hare lip was the main reason he had not done well at school, especially as his mumbling always made him reluctant to speak, which, in turn, had not helped with his grades. He had left school early and had looked for jobs where he could just be on his own, not surrounded by too many people with whom he would have to interact or talk. The job of toilet attendant suited him as he could just go about his business without meeting too many colleagues or having to interact with people, and he had now worked cleaning toilets in this part of Brixton for many years. People did indeed largely leave him alone in his job, as they were doubly repulsed: first by the terrible scar from the botched hare lip operation and, second, by the fact that he cleaned other people's shit, piss and vomit, which most people found deeply repugnant. As a result, apart from the odd staring child needing the toilet and pointing a finger at his lip and asking their mum why 'the man looked so horrible', people tended to avoid looking at him. Indeed, when they entered the toilets they just saw him as part of the accessories, more like a moving urinal or toilet bowl, a 'thing' and a freak rather than a human being.

But that suited Joe. He could work away in anonymity, scrape away at stubborn clumps of hardened shit, rub off persistent stains of piss, or brush away dried remnants of vomit, and not be bothered by anyone. Indeed, toilets were not spaces where people tended to linger, apart from the odd drug addicts who saw toilets as a place of refuge from the police where they could inject themselves away from prying eyes, or piss-heads who occasionally fell asleep in their puddles of vomit. Most of the time people just went in, did their business, and left as quickly as possible, often without washing their hands.

Yes, the work was awful, smelly and repetitive, but Joe had developed the knack of forgetting that he was scraping away remnants of human waste, switching off while surrounded by nauseating miasmas, and managing to be almost oblivious to his surroundings. Only occasionally was he brought back to reality while working, for example by the elderly granny who had soiled her pants with sudden diarrhoea and whose pleading eyes were hoping that Joe had not seen her predicament, by the crying young boy who had pissed himself and did not want his mother to pull down his trousers to clean him up in front of somebody else (but with the boy still managing all the while to stare at Joe's scar with wide-open eyes), by the drug addict who collapsed in front of him from an overdose with a heroin needle still stuck in his arm, or by the drunken man with a bulbous red nose vomiting pasta vongole remains onto the floor Joe had just meticulously cleaned. The worst downside of the job was that the salary was shit (literally speaking), and this was the reason why he could only afford to rent his awful bedsit in one of Brixton's most decrepit housing estates. But he was getting by, had just about enough money for food and a telly, although he knew that he would never be able to afford a car or fancy holidays.

But, thanks to the machine that had miraculously appeared in his room, today was somehow different. Joe had the feeling that the machine, with its mysterious appearance and its strange, ethereal, alien and other-worldly metallic sheen, would change his life. It could not be a coincidence that the machine had appeared in his flat. Did it not suggest that some greater destiny awaited him? As a result, Joe's senses were more alert on that day, and, for the first time in years he was more keenly aware of people around him and his surroundings (but also more aware of the awful smells surrounding him). He even spent some time during lunch break (after having assiduously washed his hands as usual) chatting to one of his young colleagues who was eager to talk about his new girlfriend, a type of mindless chit-chat Joe almost never engaged in.

But in the afternoon, the time was starting to drag. Would the day never finish? Joe was so distracted by thoughts about the machine that, for the first time, he failed to completely remove the remnants of a large diarrhoea stain on one of the less accessible toilet bowls in Toilet 12 near

Brixton's Tesco's 24h supermarket. He just was not able to concentrate on his job today, and after a while he had given up scrubbing the smelly stain. Today he just could not be bothered to complete the job. Joe knew that his boss, a fat, burly man who lacked compassion and often made bad jokes, would probably tell him off the next day, but he did not care. He just wanted to be near the machine which stood cool and inviting in the middle of his room back home, just waiting for him. Although he knew that on this day he had done a much worse job than usual, he somehow knew that his life would be different from now on. The machine would make sure of that.

6

Joe's mood was definitely different today. Normally, on his way home from work he would stare absent-mindedly at the dirty pavement, in order to avoid seeing the bleak council housing estates on either side, which seemed to engulf him with their ugly and menacing presence. But today was different. Walking home, he found the energy to look up into the grey London sky, and even the odd scrawny pigeon flying by, or the passing of a grey cloud pregnant with rain, seemed to cheer him up. Even the usually dreary act of shopping for groceries in the grimy and run-down corner shop close to his flat was less of a chore than usual, although he thought that the prices of products seemed to have gone up again. And instead of creeping up the stairs to his seventh floor flat (the lift was of course broken and had been out of action for years), tired and bent over after a hard-day's work, today he sprinted up the stairs with a spring in his step and ran towards his front door. He unlocked the door and went inside. He stood and stared at the gleaming machine with immense relief. There it was! It was still there! It had not been a dream or a mirage! It was still at the same spot where he had left it in the morning, beautiful and mysterious. *My machine ... mine, mine, mine ...*

In a flash, Joe had taken off his work clothes and had changed into a t-shirt and lose, comfortable jogging trousers, without taking his eyes off the machine for a second while he changed. He stepped slowly towards the machine und glanced over the rim at the opening at the top. The gaping black hole was still there, staring back at him with utter rimless blackness and a sense of infinity, luring him, calling and beckoning him to come closer. With wide open eyes, as if in trance, Joe pushed his hand forward into the black opening. But nothing happened. All he could feel was an ice-cold nothingness enveloping his hand, tugging at it, luring his hand further in. With some effort Joe withdrew his hand and looked at it. It felt ice-cold but otherwise appeared to be unaffected by having been inserted into the black void.

Joe stared at the machine for a little while, not knowing what to do. Then he had an idea. He went to his kitchenette and retrieved a dirty spoon from the sink. Again he moved his hand holding the spoon towards the black opening at the top of the machine, feeling a waft of ice-cold air as his hand hovered over the opening. He opened his hand and let the spoon drop into the black emptiness. The spoon disappeared without a sound, nothing could be seen. The spoon had been swallowed completely by the black nothingness. Joe peered into the hole, but he could see nothing but blackness.

Suddenly Joe heard a faint jingling near his feet. Had the spoon fallen out at the bottom? He bent down to investigate, and saw a brand-new twenty-pence coin lying on the floor. Joe kneeled on the wooden floor and inspected the bottom of the machine more closely. Only now did he detect a small slit at the foot of the machine, almost at floor level. *The twenty-pence coin must have come out of this slit?*, Joe wondered.

Quickly, Joe scanned his room. On a dusty shelf lay a sports car magazine he had bought years ago, and which he glanced at occasionally when he dreamt about owning a car in future. He had not looked at it for a while, indeed he had almost forgotten about it. He wiped the dust from the cover, carried it over to the machine and, as with the spoon, dropped it into the black opening. Again the object disappeared without a trace. After a few seconds a slightly louder jingling could be heard on the wooden floor. Now a brand new fifty-pence coin, a five-pence coin and a one-pence coin lay at his feet. Stunned, Joe grabbed the coins and piled them up next to the first twenty-pence coin on the small table below the window. Somehow he had just made 76 pence just by throwing junk into the machine!

Joe sat down on his creaking bed in deep thought. Probably he had never thought so hard in all his life, his head almost began to spin from so much thinking! Finally he stood up and took out of the shopping bag the tin of baked beans he had just bought at the corner shop. The price label was still visible on the tin: £1.09. He took the tin to the machine, waited a moment, and then let the tin drop into the black opening. With an object as heavy as this, Joe expected to hear something, but the tin disappeared without a sound. *Shame about the baked beans!*, Joe thought with a wry smile, but he was not seriously worried about his evening meal. A few seconds elapsed and, again, a jingling could be heard at his feet. He bent down and found coins to the value of £1.09.

Joe's whole face was beaming. Now he had proof that in his bedsit was a machine that could convert any object into money. And not only that. The machine seemed to be able to gauge an object's exact value, whether it was second hand, heavily used, or new. And it spat out real money, money that he so desperately needed, money that could change his miserable life! The sense of excitement he had felt all day about the machine having the potential to change his life had, indeed, been vindicated.

7

Late that evening Joe's already scantly furnished bedsit was empty of almost all movable objects. Everything that could be moved and carried to the machine and that fitted into the yawning black hole at the top had been fed into the machine: his two pillows, a few tattered books, his slippers, most of the kitchen cutlery, rusty pots and pans, cups, a few glasses, plates, towels, a bar of soap, shampoo. Even the few wooden shelves he'd had on the wall, which had been too large to fit through the opening, had been hacked to bits by Joe and fed to the machine.

Apart from the baked beans tin fed to the machine earlier, Joe had nonetheless kept the groceries he had bought earlier. While wolfing down a few sandwiches, Joe thought that, based on the experience with the baked beans tin earlier, there was no point in getting a refund from the machine on groceries he had just bought. That surely made no sense! But he'd had no qualms about feeding any of the other moveable objects from his room into the machine. It was simply too much fun hearing the constant jingling of coins gushing out of the slit at the foot of the machine.

Now Joe just sat there on his bed, soaked in sweat from his exertions. Apart from the groceries, his bed, a few pieces of cutlery, and the small table under the window were the only objects he had not fed to the machine. The coins the machine had spat out – and it seemed to only produce coins, not bank notes – lay in a pile next to him on the bed. They were shiny new coins of all denominations available in the UK, from shiny-brassy one-pence coins to golden-silvery two-pound coins. Only a few objects, such as two of his books, his alarm clock, and, strangely, an old metal kettle he had found in one of the deepest recesses of the cupboard under the sink, had been valuable enough to make the machine produce two-pound coins. Most of the other objects he had fed to the machine had only been worth a few pence. Not being good at maths, Joe struggled to add up the amount of money he now had, but after several attempts and after piling the coins into heaps of equal value on his bed, he had finally worked out that he had made £327.78 altogether. Joe had never seen so many coins in one heap. Joe smiled, and in his elation he even let the tip of his tongue scrape over the stubbly edge of the scar on his upper lip without feeling repulsed.

He lay down in bed, surrounded by collapsing heaps of coins. Because he was very tired he fell asleep immediately. This time he had no nightmares. Instead, he dreamt about things he had never dreamt before: about cars, women and holidays; about not having to scrape shit off toilet bowls; about expensive flat-screen TVs, gold watches and electronic gizmos; about having a second expensive operation on his upper lip by an expert who would make the scar disappear and who would also operate his upper palate to prevent him from mumbling; about learning to speak properly and addressing large crowds who avidly listened to his words; about moving out of this horrid bedsit into a nice large house in the countryside with a big garden; and about a life that would be so much better than his current one.

For the first time in years Joe was not woken up by his cheap alarm clock, as he had fed the clock into the machine (£1.89, probably a large part of this was for the AA-sized battery inside). He woke up very late and, for the first time, did not think once about going to work. *Let others clean the diarrhoea, shit, piss and vomit for a change!* He did not care anymore. For Joe a new life full of riches was beginning.

8

Joe got up and looked around his barren bedsit. He was hungry. While scoffing down a few more sandwiches with a cup of tea, Joe could not stop thinking about what else he could feed to the machine. He wanted to make more money! And he had a new idea of how to do it.

He leaned out of his window and looked down seven stories at the desolate backyard. As usual, the bottom of the yard was in shade, as it was encircled on all sides by social housing tower blocks that cut off the light. But just enough light trickled in for Joe to make out the many dustbins that had, once again, not been emptied for weeks, and the many partly burst black rubbish sacks littering the ground. He had always suspected that his neighbours were just throwing their rubbish sacks out of the window, to land on ever increasing piles in the yard. *Just like some decrepit backyard in Mumbai, Djakarta or Calcutta!*, he thought, using his limited geographical knowledge and wondering whether people in these places did indeed throw away their rubbish in such a way. The stench of rubbish emanating from the backyard was one of the reasons why Joe rarely opened his window. He could not remember when the caretaker, who was theoretically looking after this block of flats, had last been seen in the yard. *Lazy sod!*, Joe thought with disgust while closing the window again.

But Joe thought that the fact that the rubbish had not been cleared for weeks could now prove to be a blessing. He ran down the dirty staircase and went through the back door into the shadowy backyard. Looking up to make sure that nobody was watching him, he randomly picked the most accessible and least damaged rubbish sacks and returned to his flat, laden with two bags full of smelly and slimy detritus. He opened the first bag and threw its contents into the gaping black hole of the machine: plastic wrappers, banana skins, mouldy sandwich remains, plastic bottles, plenty of paper (some clean, some greasy or wet), blood-soaked tampons, empty tins and cans, rotting food remains and even a dead mouse. Several coins to the value of £45.79 fell out of the slit at the bottom of the machine. The second bag yielded £37.90. Joe was elated and a big smile appeared on his face. He was clearly on to something!

Joe worked all morning, carrying rubbish bag after rubbish bag up the stairs and into the machine. When all the black rubbish bags were gone, he transferred the waste from inside the large plastic wheely-bins (at least the rubbish he could reach and lift out) into black plastic bags and carried it upstairs. After several hours of hard work, the backyard was cleaner than ever, every bit of rubbish had been fed to the machine. Although some neighbours had looked down into the yard to see what all the commotion was about (and one had shouted abuse in Bangladeshi about the noise he was making), not one neighbour had stopped Joe from what he was doing. *Indeed, people should be happy that somebody was finally cleaning up this stinking place!*, Joe had thought while staring back at another neighbour who was looking down annoyed at him as he was just putting the last stinking pile of rubbish into a bag.

After a quick shower and a few more sandwiches, Joe spent the rest of the day counting the coins the machine had spewed out. He thought with elation about the fact that at certain points during his waste-feeding frenzy into the gaping hole, so many coins had come out of the machine that he had to brush them aside with his feet. His whole bed was now full of coins. Joe's maths was not good enough to accurately count such large piles of coins, but he estimated that he had made about £800, give or take a few quid. A fortune! This was almost as much as he made in a whole month cleaning toilets.

Exhausted, and surrounded by piles of coins, Joe lay back on his bed. For the first time in years he was happy, very happy.

9

He woke up again, soaked in sweat. It was dark outside and felt like the middle of the night, but light from a distant moon bathed the room in a mysterious silvery sheen. He must have fallen asleep amid the heaps of coins surrounding him, and the jingling of the coins on his bed must have woken him up. Had he had the nightmare again? He could not remember. In any case, he had not slept very well, probably because his neck was aching as he had fed his pillows to the machine.

The machine was faintly glistening in the moonlight, even more haunting and alluring than before. With his tired eyes, Joe could not exactly make out the contours of the machine. *Is it moving towards me?*, he thought with a shudder. But he knew that was impossible. After rubbing his eyes again, he was relieved to see that the machine stood at exactly at the same place as before, bulky, square, heavy, and looking teasingly and alluringly back at him with its silvery-metallic sheen.

Joe got up and walked over to the machine. He touched the cool metallic surface. He almost felt tenderness and love towards the machine, his machine! Gently he caressed the slightly rough shark-skin-like surface, he even knelt down and kissed it, his scarred knobbly lip feeling the coolness of the surface, his sweaty hands cautiously stroking the metallic surface. Lying on his side and wrapping his whole body around the foot of the machine, Joe fell asleep.

10

Lying on the floor next to the machine, Joe dreamt again. At first, they were pleasant dreams, dreams about his future life as a rich man, kept in wealth and comfort by the machine spitting out new coins forever. But after a while he started tossing and turning on the cold floor, and his dreams took on a nastier and more sombre hue. At first he dreamt that he was walking through a barren, snowy landscape full of dead trees. He was only wearing his pyjamas, and he was cold … bitterly cold. But then the dream turned nastier: hugging himself to ward off the cold, he saw something in the distance, half hidden by the dead trees and the flurries of snow. As he walked through the dead trees whose gnarled branches tugged at him like crooked witches' fingers, the shape in the distance took on form. It was black and about the size of a man, but with indistinct edges. Joe sensed in his dream that the black shape was evil. But he still could not see exactly what the black thing was. Although he did not want to continue walking towards it, he could not stop. Joe looked away, he did not want to approach the evil black thing, but the dream propelled him closer and closer. He turned his head away, an immense sense of dread and doom began to overwhelm him, the typical nightmarish feeling one sometimes had in a dream accompanied by the knowledge that there was no escape. *Wake up! Wake up!*, he shouted inwardly to himself, but the dream did not let him wake up.

It continued to propel him towards that indistinct black thing, towards sheer evil.

With a start, Joe woke up, but he immediately felt that his body was in a weird and unusual position, as if he was standing and bending over. His eyes were open, but he could see nothing, absolutely nothing. *Where am I?*, he wondered in panic as his senses gradually came back to life. He could feel his feet on the cold wooden floor, he could feel his stomach pushing against something hard and sharp, like the edge of a large box, and he could feel his hands clasping the rim of something. But he was gasping for air. He tried to breathe, but he could hardly suck any oxygen into his lungs out of this black nothingness. He knew he was no longer dreaming, as he could feel his body alive and alert. But this black nothingness still surrounded him.

Then he felt it. Something ice-cold was sucking him deeper into a black void, something indescribably powerful and nasty. As his hands had to clasp the rim of whatever large object he was clutching, the reality of his situation suddenly dawned on Joe: he was bending halfway down into the black hole of the machine! Half of his upper body was inside the machine's black opening, that was why he could not see or hear anything. After falling asleep at the foot of the machine, he must have sleepwalked into an upright position and bent over into the black hole.

With an almost superhuman effort Joe tried to wrench himself free from the machine. He was now panicking and very scared, as the suction of the icy black void around him intensified. The machine was trying to suck and pull him inside it! With a last desperate attempt to wrench himself free he mustered all the strength he could find in his arms and legs, and suddenly managed to tear himself from the black opening. He thought he heard a loud 'pop' as his upper body finally emerged from the black hole.

Joe took a gigantic gasp of air and collapsed onto the floor at the foot of the machine. What had happened? Had the machine tried to suck him in? Why had he not woken up before half disappearing into the black void? Feeling very scared, he looked at the machine. But everything was calm and quiet, the machine stood there in its unreal, serene, ethereal metallic beauty as if nothing had happened. Completely exhausted Joe staggered to his bed, lay down, and went back to sleep immediately.

11

When he woke up late in the morning, Joe felt well rested. He rubbed his eyes and looked over at the machine. He vaguely remembered a nightmare he'd had in the night, something about a forest, but he could not remember much else. He had the impression that he might have sleepwalked over to the machine at one point in the night, but he was no longer sure whether this in itself was part of the nightmare or whether it had happened in reality. He pressed his fingers gently to his eyes and tried to concentrate. *What was that dream about last night?*, he thought desperately, as if there was something in the deepest recesses of his mind trying to warn him that something awful had happened, and that remembering this dream was important. He rubbed his temples and concentrated hard, but he simply could not remember. He opened his eyes again, but any remnant memory of last night faded quickly, like dead leaves being cast away one by one in a sudden flurry of wind.

He shook his head and got up. He knew that any memory of his dream was now irretrievably lost, however hard he tried to concentrate. While walking towards the fridge to make breakfast, the sight of the immense pile of coins on his table brought a smile to his face.

12

Over the next few days, Joe did not think any further about the recent nightmare he'd had, and he slept well, even without his pillows. He did not think at all about going to work. *Let others clean the toilets!*, he thought happily. *With this machine I will never need to work again!*, he mused while looking lovingly at the machine.

He had used every spare minute to roam through his decrepit neighbourhood, where he had collected everything he could carry to feed into the machine. From his pile of coins, he had bought a shopping trolley on wheels at the local supermarket, which made it easier to convey gathered objects back to his flat, all the while eliciting curious stares from neighbours he met on the stairs as he awkwardly heaved the full trolley over the steps. But he did not care what his neighbours thought. With all the coins he was amassing, he would soon be out of here, away to a nicer place, away from all this decrepitude and squalor.

On his journeys through the neighbourhood he had mainly collected discarded rubbish, but he had also been curious about how much the machine would pay him for twigs, leaves, small branches, bits of bark, grass and even dog turds (which he carefully picked up with a small plastic bag). Picking up the turds reminded him briefly of his job, which already seemed like a distant memory. But in this squalid part of London greenery was very rare, as everything was concreted up in the form of ugly housing estates, awful rows of garages with huge concreted and tarmacked surfaces in front of them, and polluted car-jammed roads. This left hardly any room for trees, shrubs or patches of grass. But, luckily, one of the nearby parks provided ample material.

While Joe had not thought much about how the machine 'decided' what to pay out for individual objects, he was nonetheless surprised that it seemed to pay an inordinate amount for fresh plants. For example, a freshly cut branch with green shoots from one of the oak trees in the park generated £47.23 in coins; a small leafless twig, possibly from a rowan tree, still yielded £3.87; and even just one individual beech leaf paid out 96 pence. But the monetary yield varied hugely between different items. Dead leaves, for example, only yielded a few pence at most, but, most astonishingly, one of the fresh dog turds he fed to the machine yielded £25.40!

But with his relatively simple mind, Joe did not dwell long on the philosophical implications of how the machine valued objects. All he cared about was that the machine continued to spit out brand-new coins. There now appeared to be an endless supply of objects from the streets and the parks near him that could be fed into the machine. In the evenings, after an exhausting day's work of carrying several loads (comprised mainly of plant material) in his trolley to the machine, Joe usually just lay on his bed. There he played with his new coins, which he let gently trickle from his hands onto his tummy with a pleasing jingling sound, or he sorted the new coins into individual piles of same denomination for easier counting. The best time was when he counted how much he had earned on the day. His small table was now buckling so much under the weight of coins that Joe had started stacking up piles of coins on the floor. After a few days of collecting and feeding objects into the machine, Joe reckoned that he had now amassed coins to the value of about £5000, a formidable fortune in his eyes.

13

One evening, it must have been a little over a week since the machine had first appeared, Joe lay on his bed, thinking. He was not ready for sleep yet. Absent-mindedly he stared at the mouldy ceiling and, not for the first time, started concocting plans about his future. Casting his eyes at the huge pile of coins, he knew that he would soon need to convert the coins into banknotes, so that he could more easily carry and stash away his riches. *Imagine if somebody walked into my flat, my awful landlord, for example, and saw all these piles of coins?*, he thought slightly worried. But how could he carry all these coins without raising suspicion? And he would also have to go to many different banks so as not to raise their suspicion about where all these coins were coming from. *Shame that the machine does not spit out banknotes!*, Joe briefly thought. But he quickly dismissed this thought, as he did not want to criticise his lovely machine for one second. His machine that made him so rich! Who cared whether it was coins or bank notes, as long as it was money!

Joe thought about his job and his colleagues. The city council had not yet been in touch about him missing work for over a week, but Joe knew that it would not be long until they sacked him. But he did not care! Even if they sacked him tomorrow, he now had enough money to live on for months, even if he moved to a more expensive place. And there were endless supplies of greenery from the park to be fed into the machine, guaranteeing a steady income. If he lived somewhere in the countryside, how much 'material' he would have there from woods, hedges and fields to feed into the machine! Or he could move near to a waste dump which would provide endless amounts of rubbish to feed to the machine for years to come. People would be happy for all that waste to 'disappear'! The prospects seemed endless. And as long as he could find a way to convert the coins into banknotes or pay them directly into his bank account he would soon be a millionaire!

Still staring vacantly at the ceiling, Joe focused his thoughts on leaving this awful bedsit and the squalor of this housing estate. But he would then have to transport the machine to a new place. That was the trickiest part of any change to his current life, as he had no car, no driver's licence, and no friends with cars or vans who could help him. And if he asked a friend or acquaintance to help, they would know about the machine! So that was no good. If he moved, he had to do it by himself. So, first, he had to check whether the machine could be moved at all. The machine looked very heavy, although Joe was still not sure what it was made of. Although the surface looked like metal with its shark-skin like surface, was it actually metal or was it maybe some kind of new plastic that was quite light?

Although Joe was tired from another hard day's work gathering branches and leaves and feeding them to the machine, he felt that he had to find out immediately whether the machine could be moved at all. He got up from his bed and walked over to the machine which stood as usual still, glistening, ominous, but also slightly threatening, in the fading light. But a thought suddenly occurred to Joe. What if moving the machine stopped it from functioning properly? *After all, I still don't know how it came to suddenly appear in my room?*, he wondered not for the first time. *Did it just appear by itself or did somebody place it there? But who would that somebody be, and why have they not made themselves known to me? Will it still spit out coins if I move it from its current place?* His head began to spin again from all this thinking. All these questions and no answers!

He stood right next to the machine, gaping into the black opening at the top. He put his arms around the outside of the square body of the machine and tried to lift or move it, but nothing happened. The cool and rough surface felt almost pleasing to the touch of his sweaty hands. He tightened his grip, and with all the muscle power he could muster from his thighs and arms he pulled and pushed the machine. But it did not budge an inch. He tried to extend his grip around the back corners of the machine to get better purchase, while still pushing, heaving, shoving and pulling. As he had to bend down more with this new grip, his head was now hovering over the black opening. An indescribable coldness emanated from the black, gaping hole. His grasp loosened a little, and his head hovered ever closer towards the opening. Joe felt as if he was being hypnotised, he felt as if he was being sucked irretrievably into the black abyss.

Just as Joe's head hovered dangerously close to the gaping hole and was about to disappear into it, he opened his eyes wide, and with a loud cry and an almost inhuman effort he managed to prize himself away from the machine. Losing his balance, he fell backwards onto the floor with a loud thud. What had happened? Had the machine tried to lure him into the hole? Why would it do this? Somehow this situation reminded Joe vaguely of something, but he was not sure what. Was it a memory or a dream, something he had already seen in the darkest recesses of his mind? But, unable to pin down these memories further, he brushed these thoughts aside and focused again on the present. He obviously had gone too close to the opening while trying to lift the machine off the ground. He would have to be much more careful in future. But, worst of all, his plans to attempt to move the machine were in jeopardy. Under no circumstances should he try to lift the machine again or get his head anywhere near the opening.

In the semi-darkness he looked at the machine with different eyes, more cautious, more sceptical, like a cat after being badly singed by a burning flame. He was still very shaken about what had just happened and was not sure what to do next. Keeping a respectful distance from the machine, Joe strode around the room in deep thought. Was the machine dangerous? For the first time he wondered whether he should maybe even consider moving out, rent another room, and just leave the machine in here to produce money while he slept elsewhere?

One thing he was now certain about was that there was no way that he could move the machine out of the room on his own. Unless he rented another room to sleep in, for the foreseeable future he was stuck in this shabby, grimy, dirty and small bedsit, despite all the money piled up next to him. But, as long as nobody came into his flat and saw the machine, maybe he could amass so much money in a year or so that he would no longer need the machine?

Probably the first thing to do would be to get a driver's licence, then buy a van so that he could transport material to be fed into the machine more easily and on a more industrial scale. Yes, that was it, that was the way forward! *Don't worry too much about moving the machine, or moving out. Just make as much money as you can in the next few weeks and months, pay the coins slowly into your bank account or change them gradually into bank notes, get a driver's licence and a van, and then we'll see what we should do next!*, Joe thought, pleased with himself. As he made his way back to bed, he had already almost forgotten how a few moments ago he had half hung over the black ice-cold opening of the machine. Very tired, Joe lay down again on his bed. Although at the back of his mind warning sounds were still ringing, he was happy with his new plans. He knew that any problems could be sorted out, but all he wanted to do now was to sleep …

14

It was the middle of the night when a terrible nightmare woke Joe up again. Still half asleep, the thought about the dream made Joe shudder with fear, but, again, he could not remember what he had dreamt. He felt cold sweat pouring down his face, his pyjamas were clammy with sweat. He rubbed his eyes, opened them properly for the first time … and realised, terrified, that he was not in his bed but standing right next to the machine!

Panicked, he realised that he must have sleepwalked again. His hands rested on the cool metallic surface. Was he still dreaming or was he awake? His right hand touched the edge of the black opening, and then dived into it. No, all of this was real, he obviously was not dreaming. He could feel the black ice-cold nothingness caressing the skin on his hand, making the tiny hairs on his forearm stand up. Now his upper body arched forward towards the opening. *What am I doing?*, his numbed and panicked mind tried to rationalise. *What is happening? Am I going mad?* But a force stronger than himself pulled him towards the gaping black hole.

In the deepest recesses of his mind something clicked. With a jolt, Joe suddenly remembered the awful nightmares he'd had before, the first one in the night when the machine had first appeared, the second one just a few days ago, and the third one just a few moments ago. They were all the same dream, the same nightmare! Horrified, he remembered dreaming that the machine had tried to suck him into the opening and that he had to muster all his strength to wrench himself free from the sucking, luring, black abyss. He now even remembered the dreadful time when he'd had to pull himself free from the machine, after waking up with his upper body inside the machine. It had not been a dream. It had all been real! Remembering all this made Joe panic even more. Had the nightmare been an evil harbinger of what was going to happen to him? Had his subconscious sent him warning signs all along, and had he just not been able, or willing, to read and interpret the signs? Why was he suddenly remembering these dreams now, why not earlier?

But his face still hovered over the black void. He tried to see something, anything, but what he saw was nothing … the deepest nothingness imaginable, an endless black abyss. Somehow he could not take his eyes off the black void. With the warning cries of his dreams still echoing inside his skull, he tried to stay rational, to stay in control, to fight what was happening. *The dreams have told you what will happen!*, the last dregs of his rational mind tried to tell him. *Fight it! Be strong!* But very slowly his body bent further forward, he could not help it, even if his deepest inner self tried to resist it. It was as if his body was detaching itself from his mind. *Get away, get away!*, he thought desperately, flexing his muscles in desperation.

But something bigger than anything he had ever felt before lured his body closer towards the gaping black hole, an irresistible, daunting, ice-cold and all-encompassing force. It was as if his soul was wrenched from his body and dragged into the abyss, the luring black void. Still holding on tightly to the edge of the opening with both hands, Joe wanted to shout, cry for help, alert his neighbours, but no sound escaped from his throat. It was too late. He started shaking with the effort of clinging on to the edge of the machine, but he felt his feet slowly leaving the ground, his strength failing. His head slid slowly into the black nothingness. With his last remnant willpower his hands desperately tried to cling onto the edge of the machine, but slowly his sweaty palms slipped from the rim. Without support from his arms, his whole upper body suddenly slid into the gaping opening, and a moment later Joe fell head-first into the blackness and disappeared.

After a few seconds a barely audible jingling could be heard …

Printed in Great Britain
by Amazon